For our Earth's most precious resource: our children.

www.mascotbooks.com

Robots and Other Amazing Gadgets Invented 800 Years Ago

©2022 Faisal Hossain and Qishi Zhou. All Rights Reserved. No part of this publication may be reproduced, stored in a retrieval system or transmitted in any form by any means electronic, mechanical, or photocopying, recording or otherwise without the permission of the author.

Photo Credits
Stopwatch, page 6: Paddle.com
Four-cylinder engine, page 8: wavecaplet
Piston moving backward and forward, page 9: Sketchplanations.com
Whistling kettle, page 10: Paddle.com
Amusement park tilting water bucket, page 11: Empex Watertoys

For more information, please contact
Mascot Books, an imprint of Amplify Publishing Group:
620 Herndon Parkway #320
Herndon, VA 20170
info@mascotbooks.com

Library of Congress Control Number: 2022903862

CPSIA Code: PRT0322A
ISBN-13: 978-1-63755-385-5

Printed in the United States

Robots and Other AMAZING GADGETS

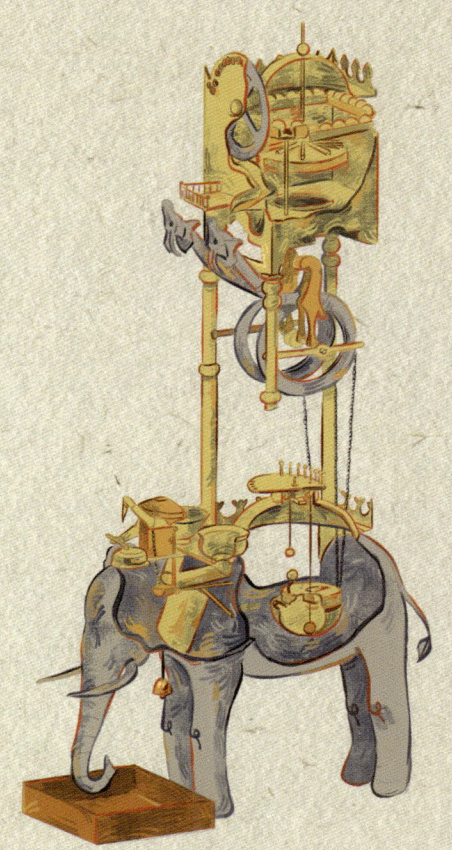

Invented 800 Years Ago

Faisal Hossain and Qishi Zhou

Illustrated by Hatice Sena Balkan

Authors' Note

In today's world, we are exposed to automation from an early age. For children who are just beginning to develop their senses and explore their new world, this is sometimes the first experience they can remember. Thanks to the internet, computers, and on-demand services, our children are perhaps more "wired" than they have been at any point in human history. The COVID-19 pandemic has accelerated this exposure to automation due to the need for online schooling. As the fifth industrial revolution creeps into all walks of life, we have wondered about the psychological effects automation may have on our children. If our children are exposed to such extensive automation from an early age, will they ever learn to appreciate or truly understand how the physical world works? Will they understand nature and the basic laws that govern the analog world we live in, or will they think that the internet has it covered?

Our curiosity about this issue led us to write this children's book when we accidentally discovered that the robot was not a modern invention. The first documented robot was invented almost 800 years ago by a polymath named Ismail Al-Jazari who lived in modern-day Iraq. Jazari predated Leonardo da Vinci and was a prolific inventor of automated devices including tea-dispensing robots, mechanical clocks, automated flutes, washing machines, and toilet cisterns, many of which are still used today. In many circles, Jazari is often called "the father of robotics and cellular automata." Our fascination with Jazari became addictive after we learned that all his inventions based on automation were created when there was no electricity, circuit boards, or diodes to control logic of an operation. Yet, Jazari found a way to automate a series of "instructions" by using water. He used concepts of hydraulics and hydrostatic forces to create his "circuit boards" running on water energy. We believe these medieval inventions provide a teaching moment for our children to help them think of the natural world at the most fundamental level, and make connections to electronic devices they are now getting increasingly exposed to.

While working on this book, we felt that if we could illustrate some of Jazari's inventions appropriately for our children and explain the basic concept behind them, they could be inspired to learn more about the physical world the analog way (without using the internet or an app). Basically, such a book could perhaps make our children want to go outside, watch, explore, and think about the everyday motions of trees, wind, birds, rivers, clouds, and how they all work. Our hope is that our children will also learn to appreciate that mastery of fundamental concepts is all we need to overcome challenges—not electricity, LCD screens, or fancy phones and apps. If the solution is physically sound at the conceptual level, it will work and do the job of automation even at a crude level.

We sought help from a variety of sources in creating this children's book. First, we had to access Jazari's modern-day rendition of his book titled *The Book of Knowledge of Ingenious Mechanical Devices* that was originally published 800 years ago and translated by Donald Hill. This book was supplemented with a more recent and wonderfully illustrated book in Turkish titled *Cezeri'nin Olağanüstü Makineleri: Herkes İçin Cezeri* by Mehmed Ali Çalışkan. Our wonderful Turkish friends Mehmet Ozcelik and Bilal Çorbacıoğlu helped translate many of Jazari's key inventions. Our other and equally wonderful friends Merve Cirisoglu and Hatice Sena Balkan (of Animatick Arts) helped illustrate inventions from a child's perspective to explain the basic concepts that rule the natural world.

In total there are eight inventions shown here. Each invention has an illustration and an explanation of how it works. They are organized from the simplest and easiest to understand, to the more complex inventions with more moving parts. Our hope is that this book will inspire children to learn about and appreciate the real world we live in as much as their laptops and phones.

Faisal Hossain and Qishi Zhou
University of Washington
Seattle, Washington, USA

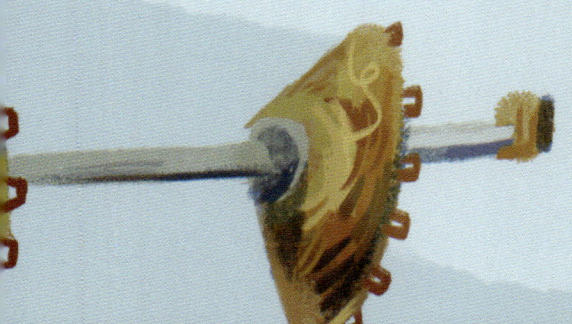

Ismail Al-Jazari was a polymath, an engineer, an artist, and a prolific inventor.

Who Invented Robots 800 Years Ago?

The inventor's name is as long as his list of inventions: Badī' az-Zaman Abu l-'Izz ibn Ismā 'Īl ibn ar-Razāz al-Jazarī. He is more commonly known as Al-Jazari, and he was born sometime during the twelfth century in northern Iraq. Considered a polymath, a mechanical engineer, and an artist, Al-Jazari is best known for his book *The Book of Knowledge of Ingenious Mechanical Devices* (in Arabic, *Kitab fi ma'rifat al-hiyal al-handasiya*). A polymath is generally someone who has a vast range of knowledge and expertise with ideas far ahead of their time, like a Renaissance person such as Leonardo da Vinci. Al-Jazari is known as "the father of robotics." Keep reading to find out why!

Water-Flowing Timer

Today, we have a timer or a stopwatch on our phones to measure a specified length of time. In the twelfth century, Al-Jazari came up with a water-flowing timer based on the concept of a sinking bowl inside a water container. He called the bowl "tarcehar," and used the principles of Archimedes and some meticulous engineering to perfect the timer for use in mechanical clocks.

To understand how Al-Jazari's timer works, think of a sinking ship, like the *Titanic*. As water seeps in the ship through the cracked hull, the ship becomes heavier and gradually sinks. If we could calculate the rate at which water seeps in, the time taken for the *Titanic* to sink completely could be calculated.

In Al-Jazari's invention, the tarcehar is a bowl with a hole in the bottom that floats in water. When water seeps into the tarcehar through the hole, this makes the tarcehar slowly descend for a specified amount of time, which can be adjusted by the size of the hole. Once the tarcehar is full, it sinks rapidly to the bottom of the water container. Al-Jazari used this timed movement to great effect as a trigger or a fuse to operate many of his more complex inventions.

Al-Jazari placed a piece of agate stone on the water intake hole at the bottom of the tarcehar bowl. First, a very small hole was drilled, and the agate stone was attached to it with wax. The tarcehar bowl was then placed in water. Due to hydrostatic pressure, water started to seep in the bowl and the hole gradually enlarged. This caused the tarcehar bowl to sink after a specified time. The role of the agate stone is to act as a trigger when the tarcehar bowl is completely sunk. With strings attached to the stone, a variety of trigger mechanisms can be devised when the tarcehar sinks. The same principle is applied to record time or generate a new motion in mechanical clocks such as the Elephant and Boat Water Clocks, also invited by Al-Jazari.

Modern-day stopwatch.

Al-Jazari's Water-Flowing Timer.

A four-cycle gear system invented by Al-Jazari.

An animal-powered, four-cycle mechanical gear to scoop water for irrigation invented by Al-Jazari.

Four-Cycle Mechanical Gear System

Al-Jazari invented an animal-powered, four-cycle gear system to scoop water from a river or well for irrigation. The concept is very similar to four-cylinder engines used in motor vehicles today, where the motion of one of the pistons rotates the crankshaft by 90 degrees, and the other pistons follow. Here, the animal turns a shaft by 90 degrees, which leads to a vertical gear to rotate and lift a scoop that naturally stays immersed in water in the well or river at a lower level.

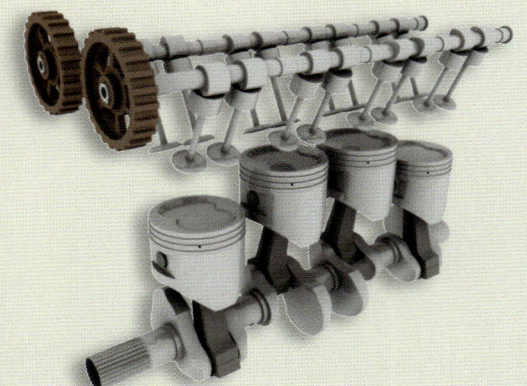

Today, four-cylinder engines are used in motor vehicles that incorporate the concept of a course-cycle gear system.

This system of gear implementation was not seen before Al-Jazari's time. Remember, Al-Jazari's inventions were made a few centuries before the European Renaissance and the Industrial Revolution. Al-Jazari built the four-cycle gear system having to consider angular motion and phased difference. In fact, today's simple concept of rotary motion leading to linear motion of a piston that is used widely in vehicles was actually first invented by Al-Jazari.

Piston moving backward and forward based on circular motion.

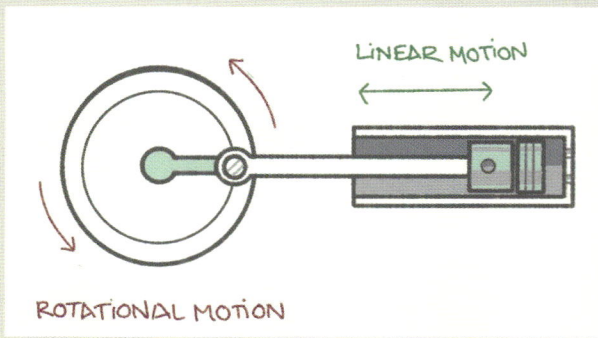

Automatic Directional Control System

Al-Jazari came up with a water-based directional control system that surprised even himself! In his original design book he called this invention "strange and surprising." Today, directional control systems are used in many applications to direct or stop the flow of pressurized air or oil to an appliance such as an HVAC system.

The idea behind this invention is to have water flow into two different streams, and the flowrate of each can be controlled as desired. One of the streams leads to a scoop that is paired with another at 90 degrees with each other. The other stream can be drained to a separate pipe. As the scoop collects water, it becomes heavier and starts to rotate downward, which causes the empty scoop to rotate upward. A point will come when the scoop with water will reach the position where all the water must drain at the same instant when the other scoop reaches a horizontal position under the other stream to start collecting water. This process repeats itself, but in the opposite direction after a fixed interval of time, as long as water is maintained in the two streams. The interval of time can be programmed according to flowrates and size of the scoop. With differing flow rates or scoop sizes, two different intervals of time can be made part of the repeat cycle for direction control.

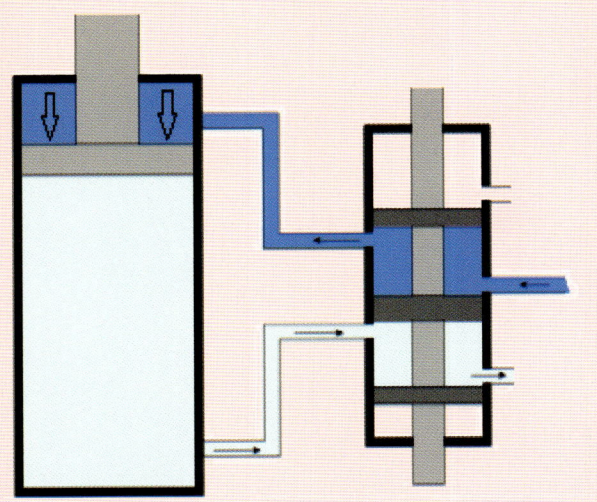

Directional control of water flow simplified. When the piston is pushed down, water shown in blue flows from right to left from a tank on the right side. At the same time, water shown in light gray flows in the opposite direction (from left to right). With such a system, we can have water flowing in opposite directions and use it to start, stop, or withdraw flow from an appliance.

A water-based directional control system invented by Al-Jazari. As long as water keeps flowing into the two different streams, any interval of time for changing direction from clockwise to counterclockwise can be programmed based on the size of the scoop.

A water horn invented by Al-Jazari that works on the basis of pressurizing air with water.

Water Horn

Al-Jazari invented the concept of pressurizing air with water to create sound that he used in a horn, and later in perpetual flutes playing alternate notes. It is quite ingenious, yet simple if you think about it. In today's world, we can think of this as a loud whistling kettle.

Water flows into an airtight container by gravity. As water rises inside the container, it pressurizes the air inside. There is a horn attached to the container on one end. This horn is basically a valve that lets air out only when it reaches a certain pressure. With water collecting in the container, the time it takes for the horn to blow and how often it sounds can be meticulously timed. The horn can even be set to go off at fixed intervals by having another pipe to siphon off the water.

A whistling kettle that boils water uses the concept of pressurized air and water vapor flowing through a small opening to create a sound, and announces that the water is boiling.

Automatic Tilting Buckets For Alternate Motion

Without realizing that he was pioneering "control theory" that had not yet been invented 800 years ago, Al-Jazari used water to control the perpetual motion of tilting buckets and control alternate motion. Today, we see such examples in water amusement parks where tilting water buckets splash a large volume of water once they are filled.

It's another simple, yet genius concept. There are two tilting buckets placed next to each other like a balance. The buckets are shaped like the front hull of a ship and held with a pivot. Above them is a pipe carrying water that is pivoted in the center. Water will flow through this pipe only to one of the buckets when it is not balanced. The placement of the pivot for the bucket and the shape of the bucket are designed such that when the bucket is full, it never tilts over backwards due to a resting block below. When the bucket is filled with water carried by the tilted pipe above, balance is lost, causing the bucket to tilt forward and empty. Two actions are triggered with this draining motion. First, the rotation of the bucket causes the pipe to tilt to the other direction and start filling the other bucket. After a fixed interval of time, the water that drains from each bucket as it empties can be channeled in alternating directions to operate a variety of operations, such as alternating fountains or flutes.

Today, you can see giant tilting water buckets in amusement parks that automatically splash water down once they are full.

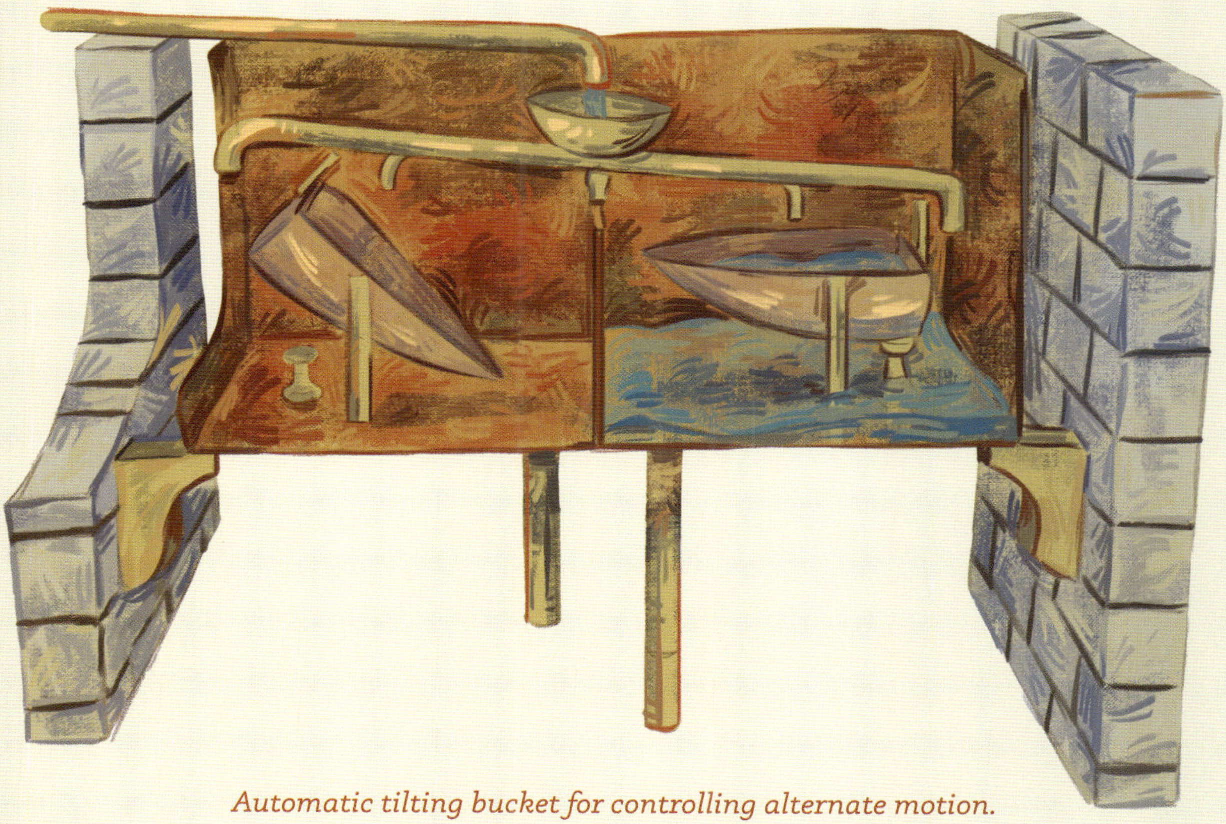

Automatic tilting bucket for controlling alternate motion.

Application of automatic tilting bucket for an alternately flowing fountain.

Automatic priest for blood measurement.

Inner workings of the automatic priest.

Automatic Priest For Blood Measurement

Al-Jazari also delved into medicine. One of his ingenious inventions is the automatic priest for blood measurement. During medieval times, bloodletting was a common medical practice in the Middle East, performed often by monks and priests. In the modern world, such a concept is used to monitor blood flow out of one's body during a blood donation drive.

To keep track of how much blood was drained from the patient, Al-Jazari devised a flat bowl that collects drops of blood that drain through the hole in the center and collect in a vertical tube. Inside the tube, there is a float connected by a string around a horizontal pulley and a counterweight at the other end. As more blood droplets accumulate in the tube, the float rises, causing the pulley to rotate steadily. The rotary motion of the pulley causes a miniature priest to rotate along the circumference of the bowl that is graduated with markings. The entire device appears as if the priest is automatically calculating the amount of blood that was let by pointing his stick to the specific marking. The sensitivity and precision of this device can be controlled by designing the right set of pulley, float, and diameter of the bowl.

Elephant Water Clock

This is perhaps Al-Jazari's most famous invention. What makes this invention unique is that the clock is built on a perfect integration of many small mechanical devices that work in unison to produce an entertaining experience of time—800 years ago! The key concept is based on equal timing that can be controlled to the beginning of every half hour and the minutes in between.

The elephant water clock performs its timing with the slow sinking of a bowl (called tarcehar—also used in the water-flowing timer) inside the belly of the elephant. The clock gets its power from the force created at the time of the sinking of the bowl, and the potential energy of the balls that is released. As the bowl sinks at the end of half an hour, one of the bronze spheres standing in a row in the closed chamber at the top of the clock falls, and visual movements are formed.

Elephant Water Clock.

Floating in the pool inside the belly of the elephant, the tarcehar bowl slowly sinks for half an hour by taking water from the hole on its bottom, while the clerk on the elephant's back slowly turns and shows the minutes with a pen in his hand through rotary motion, caused by the linear motion of the bowl sinking. At the end of half an hour, as the bowl descends and sinks, the bird on the top turns. At the same time, the sitting ruler above raises his hand on the beak of the falcon on his side, and holds the beak of the falcon on the other side with his other hand. All these motions are triggered by the conversion of linear motion to rotary motion of the sinking of the bowl and the release of balls.

A spherical ball falls from the beak of the freed falcon into the open mouth of the snake, which is ready to devour the falcon. When the snake's heavy head lowers, the ball is left in one of the two vases on the elephant's shoulder, and a gong sound comes out of the vase. When the snake's head gets lighter, it slowly rises, while the clerk returns to its former place. The snake that rises up also pulls the sinking bowl up and, thanks to its hinged tie, drains its water and makes it ready for the next half hour. In the meantime, the spherical ball enters the neck of the elephant after the vase, and the elephant driver hits the metal cap on the top of the elephant once with a mallet with one hand, and a pickaxe with the other.

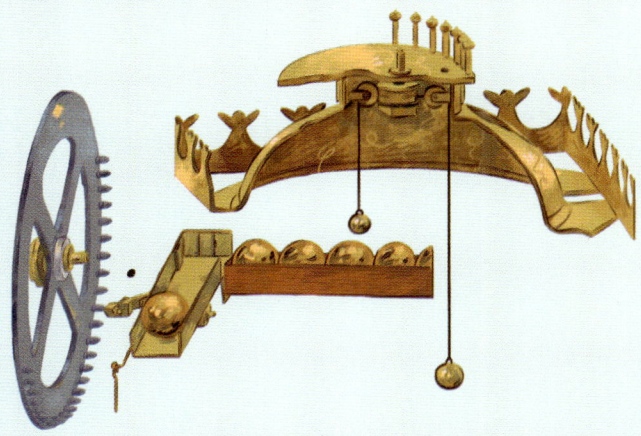

Spherical balls in the Elephant Water Clock that travel due to potential energy and cause rotary motion.

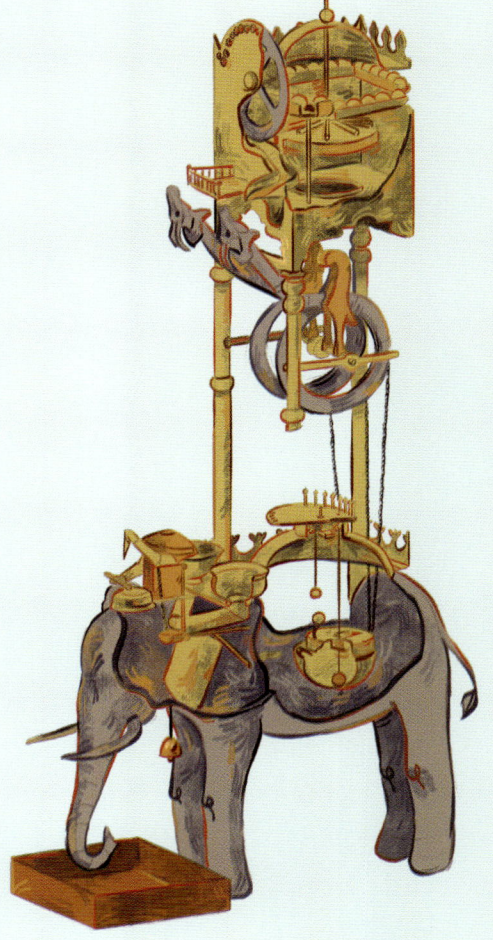

Inner components of the Elephant Water Clock.

A Robot That Washes Your Hands And Face

Al-Jazari made a fun, childlike robot that can wash the user's hands and face! This invention is one of the most striking of his creations.

When the robot is activated, a bird seated on top of a water jug held by the robot sings for a while. This singing is designed as a "waiting period" for the person to prepare for getting washed. When the singing ends, water starts to flow from the jug automatically. When the flowing water is about to stop completely, the robot extends a comb and a mirror from his hand to the person who just washed their hands and face. The system has three basic mechanical elements: a singing bird (sound created with pressurized water), a self-activating water fountain, and a mirror/comb extender arm. The robot executes the actions of singing, watering, and mirror/comb extension in sequence using the flow of water.

In order for the system to work, water is used in this robot, which the operator fills into the tank in its body through the hole under the robot's hat in the back room. When the operator brings the robot for public use, they turn a small knob on the neck of the robot. After that, the water inside the robot fills the jug gradually, causing the air trapped in the jug to pressurize and create a bird-sounding whistle through a nozzle. After a while, when the jug is full, water begins to flow from another nozzle, which acts as a siphon. When the water in the jug empties, the robot extends the comb and the mirror with the other hand. This movement is triggered by a float located inside the jug.

About Faisal Hossain

Faisal Hossain is a teacher who enjoys interacting with students at all levels and disciplines as part of his day job as a professor in the Department of Civil and Environmental Engineering at the University of Washington. His night job, to which he devotes an equal amount of energy, is about filmmaking and the communication of science. He uses these to build bridges between communities and solve pressing problems for society. His research group at the University of Washington focuses on improving the quality of life in challenging environments through the application of science, technology, engineering, and math (STEM), with a focus on the supply of water, energy, and food. He initiated the nation's first Engineering Student Film Contest at the University of Washington in 2017, which is a biannual student film festival for STEM majors as a way to explore the arts.

About Qishi Zhou

Qishi Zhou is an electrical engineering graduate student at the University of Washington, and an alumnus of the University of Minnesota, Twin Cities, where he completed his bachelor's degree in computer science. His research interests include satellites communication, aeronautics, and astronautics. He loves building robots and automation that serve society and solve problems. He most recently designed a rover called "HydroCUB" for the Washington State Department of Transportation to inspect culvert conditions to help fish swim through. His dream is to use his engineering knowledge to shape the world. In his spare time, he enjoys scuba diving, making fun gadgets, and is a private pilot and film photographer.

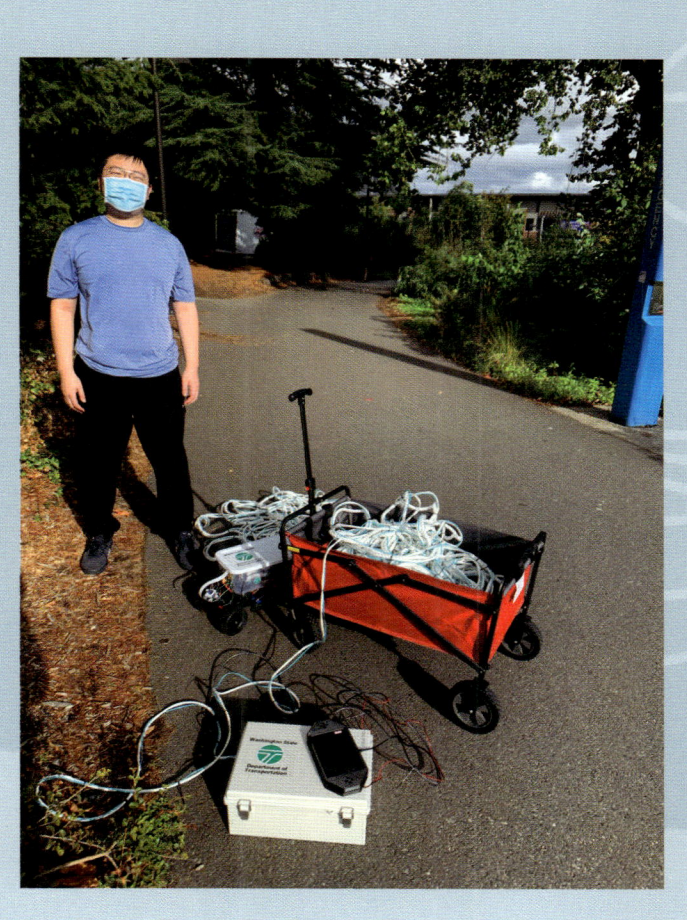